STICK DOG

CRASHES A PARTY

STICK DOG

CRASHES A PARTY

By Tom Watson

HARPER

An Imprint of HarperCollinsPublishers

Stick Dog Crashes a Party

Copyright © 2018 by Tom Watson

Illustrations by Ethan Long based on original sketches by Tom Watson

All rights reserved. Printed in the United States of America.

No part of this book may be used or reproduced in any manner whatsoever without written permission except in the case of brief quotations embodied in critical articles and reviews. For information address HarperCollins Children's Books, a division of HarperCollins Publishers, 195 Broadway, New York, NY 10007.

www.harpercollinschildrens.com

Library of Congress Control Number: 2017954084

ISBN 978-0-06-241096-2

Typography by Jeff Shake

18 19 20 21 22 CG/LSCH 10 9 8 7 6 5 4 3 2 1

First Edition

To MEJ

(IWTASD)

TABLE OF CONTENTS

CHAPTER 1

MAY I LICK YOUR NOSE?

It was cool outside as the night grew dark. But it was warm inside Stick Dog's pipe as he and his friends came closer together.

Stick Dog, Karen, Poo-Poo, and Stripes formed a circle around Mutt. They wanted dessert—and they hoped Mutt might have something.

"Just give a couple of good shakes, Mutt," Stick Dog encouraged.

"Okay," Mutt said. He was, of course, happy to help the group, but you could tell he wasn't confident there would be a sweet treat in his fur that they could share.

Mutt shook.

Several things flew out, including a pencil stub, half a slipper, two bottle caps, a shoestring, and an old paper napkin.

"Nothing," Poo-Poo said after quickly examining all the stuff that lay scattered about Mutt.

"Bummer," Karen said.

Stripes just sighed. And then her stomach grumbled.

Mutt was clearly disappointed that he let down his friends. He hung his head. And when he did, a small red-and-white packet fell from the thick fur behind his neck.

"What's that?" Karen asked, and came closer. She put her front right paw gingerly on the packet. "It feels funny. It's squishy."

"It's squishy?" asked Stripes.

"Yeah. Squishy."

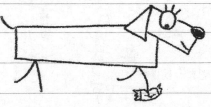

Stripes pressed her paw against the packet, felt the squishiness, and giggled.

Stick Dog was curious about the thing—and he hoped that, perhaps, this small squishy red-and-white packet would distract them from their lack of dessert. They had found a whole package of hot dog buns by the playground earlier in the day. Their bellies were relatively full for the night. They simply wanted something sweet before sleep.

Stick Dog asked, "Where did you find this interesting packet, Mutt?"

"It was in a crumpled-up Burger King bag that I found on the side of Highway 16 a few days ago," Mutt answered. He then quickly added, "But there were no hamburgers inside. Just this squishy thing and a couple of napkins."

Stick Dog nodded.

"It's fun!" Karen said. "It's squishy—and it gurgles when you touch it."

Poo-Poo asked, "Can I see?"

Mutt, Karen, and Stripes were happy to oblige his request. They each backed one step away while Poo-Poo came two steps closer.

He pressed a paw gently against the packet. He felt it squish—and heard it squelch. He exclaimed, "Neat!"

"Burger King is a restaurant," Stick Dog said quietly. He twisted his head a bit and raised his right eyebrow slightly. He was obviously trying to figure something out. "If it came from a restaurant, then—"

But Stick Dog didn't get the chance to finish his sentence.

That's because, at that precise moment, Poo-Poo pressed his paw down harder on the packet.

Too hard.

The packet burst open.

And sprayed red stuff everywhere.

Then several things happened at once:

Poo-Poo leaped into the air, arching his back quickly to get away from the spraying red terror. Stripes and Mutt jerked away. Karen shuddered but did not move. She had taken a direct hit on her little dachshund nose. She stared cross-eyed at the great red glop that had settled there.

"It's blood!" screamed Poo-Poo in midair. After he landed half a second later, he added, "Whatever was in that packet pierced Karen! She's bleeding!"

Stripes suddenly began to search Stick Dog's pipe. She swung her head left and right. She flipped the old couch cushion that Stick Dog slept on. There was nothing under it.

"Stick Dog?!" Stripes yelled.

"Yes?"

"Where are your emergency medical supplies?!"

"My what?"

"Your emergency medical supplies!" Stripes panted and then looked under the couch cushion again. There was still nothing there. "Karen is bleeding to death! Didn't you hear Poo-Poo?! We need medical supplies! Somebody boil some water! We need bandages! Get me your X-ray machine! Where's your defibrillator?! Mutt! Can you shake something out of your fur that will help?!"

"Like what, Stripes?"

"I don't know!" Stripes screamed. She was in a real panic. "A chain saw! An ambulance! Anything!"

Mutt wanted to help. So he started to shake.

"Poo-Poo's right," Karen whispered as she stood absolutely stone-still. She stared at that red glop on her nose. "I'm bleeding."

Stick Dog shook his head at this complete overreaction by his friends. He knew he had to calm down Stripes most of all. But he just had to ask something first.

"Stripes?" Stick Dog asked slowly. "Why

would you need a chain saw? I don't think of chain saws as medical equipment."

"Her nose, Stick Dog, her nose!" Stripes screamed. She was not calmed by Stick Dog's demeanor. "We might have to cut it off and glue it back on! She might need a nose job!"

Mutt seemed encouraged by this for some reason and began to shake even more vigorously.

"Well, I'm not having any luck with the chain saw or the ambulance," he said after a few seconds. "But I might have some glue in here to reattach Karen's nose after we cut it off with the chain saw. I think I found a bottle of glue behind the school a few months ago."

Stick Dog realized more direct intervention was necessary.

"Everybody stop," he said kindly, but firmly. "Karen is not bleeding. She's not hurt."

"I'm not?" asked Karen.

"I don't think so. You only see blood when you're hurt. Like when you get a bad cut or a scrape or something," Stick Dog said. There was something about the way he spoke that soothed the others. He seemed quite sure of himself. Mutt stopped shaking. Poo-Poo came a step closer toward Karen. Even Stripes settled a little bit. "Does anything hurt?"

Karen rolled her eyes around a bit to examine herself and then reached a conclusion. She said, "As a matter of fact, nothing hurts. Nothing at all. How did you know that, Stick Dog? I didn't even know myself."

"Just a lucky guess. I'm glad you're not hurt," Stick Dog said. "Now, I think what happened—"

Stripes wasn't completely convinced yet. She interrupted, "Then how do you explain the blood? Something shot out of that packet and smashed into Karen's nose! And made her bleed!"

"I think," Stick Dog said, "that the red stuff itself came out of the packet and splattered on Karen's nose. I think it just happens to be the color of blood."

"But what is it?" asked Karen. She was still nervous about it.

"Just give it a taste," Stick Dog said. "And find out."

"Seriously?!" exclaimed Karen. She still didn't move.

"I think it's food," Stick Dog assured. "Mutt found it in a bag from a restaurant. It's not a napkin or a fork or a spoon. It might be some kind of food. Like some sauce or something."

"Hey!" Poo-Poo exclaimed. Something had just occurred to him. "Maybe Stick Dog is right. I know he's not usually correct, but maybe—just maybe—he's onto something here."

Mutt asked, "Why do you think that, Poo-Poo?"

"Remember when we found those donuts?"
Poo-Poo asked.

His friends nodded.
They remembered
that morning easily. It was one of their
greatest feasts. They had gorged themselves
on two dozen donuts—and plenty of apples
too. They began to salivate at the memory.

"Well, remember the donut that I thought I
killed?" Poo-Poo asked. "It was just like this
packet! It had red liquid stuff inside too. And
I thought it was blood. But it wasn't! It tasted
like strawberries. It was food!"

"Jeez, then maybe Stick Dog *is* right,"
Stripes said with surprise in her voice.

"It's possible, I guess," whispered Karen. She still didn't move. "However unlikely."

Even Mutt concurred. "Old Stick Dog is right for a change, huh? Well, how about that? Good for you, Stick Dog. Good for you."

"Umm, thanks," replied Stick Dog.

"Does that red stuff smell like strawberries?" Poo-Poo asked.

"How should I know?" asked Karen.

"It's on your nose, Karen," Stick Dog said. "You should be able to smell it."

"Oh, right."

Stick Dog did not feel the need to mention

that Karen had likely been smelling that red
splotch this whole time. It was, after all,
on her nose. And she had been, you know,
breathing. He figured she was just too
freaked-out to notice.

So, he just said, "Give it a little sniff. See if
you can smell any delicious aromas."

Karen did just that.

She gave a tiny sniff and then squinted her
eyes in contemplation for a few seconds.

"It's pizza!"
Karen said excitedly.

"Pizza?" asked Poo-Poo, Stripes, and Mutt all at once.

The dogs all knew what pizza was—they had devoured five whole pizzas one night long ago.

"Well, it's *like* pizza," Karen amended. "It's like the red stuff that was under the cheese. Sort of."

Poo-Poo came a step closer and then asked a question that caught them all by surprise.

"Karen," he said. "May I lick your nose?"

CHAPTER 2

DELICIOUS RED GOO

Now, under normal circumstances,
Poo-Poo's request to lick Karen's nose
would be quite bizarre.

But these were not normal circumstances.

Imagine if you asked someone if you
could lick her nose. Let's call this person
Mildred—you know, just to give her a name.

Now, Mildred might think you are nuts. She would probably ask, "Why do you want to lick my nose?"

And if it was a similar situation, you would answer something like "Because there's a bit of food by your left nostril that I would like to taste."

Then Mildred would probably back slowly away and say something like "You are a loony-bird."

That's *probably* what this person would say. It's possible, I suppose, that Mildred trusts you completely. And if she is that kind of person, she might say something like this instead, "Well, it's kind of a strange request, but I trust you. Go ahead. Lick my nose."

If you ask someone if you can lick their nose and, like Mildred here, she allows you to lick her nose . . . well, I just think you should consider that person a really, really good friend.

So, here's an idea. At lunchtime at school, walk around and look for people with food on their noses. When you find one, ask them if you can lick his or her nose. If they say yes, then you've found a true friend.

PICK THIS ONE

FOOD

If your friend has a mustache, I wouldn't even ask. Licking the nose of someone with a mustache seems kind of gross.

Well, Karen didn't have a mustache. And she trusted Poo-Poo completely. So she said, "Go ahead."

Poo-Poo stuck his tongue out ever so carefully. It got closer to Karen's nose.

And closer.

And closer.

Until Poo-Poo's tongue touched the red splotch on her nose. He closed his eyes and then leaned his head back to concentrate on the flavor, allowing it to spread inside his mouth.

Stick Dog, Mutt, Stripes, and Karen waited to hear his observation. And Poo-Poo gave it to them.

"Karen's right," he said upon lowering his head and opening his eyes. "This red goo is reminiscent of that saucy tomato goodness we discovered on those pizzas. But there is something different here. There's plenty of tomato, that's for certain. But the other flavors—"

Poo-Poo didn't finish his observation.

That's because every one of the dogs—even Stick Dog—began searching the floor and walls of Stick Dog's pipe for other drips and drops that had sprayed from that packet. Poo-Poo didn't seem to mind and began to look for some red flavor spots too.

Karen was the last one to start looking. She took a few seconds to lick her nose first.

It didn't take long for all five dogs to lick a little drip here and a little drop there. They all agreed that the flavor was similar to the tomato sauce they had tasted long ago.

And that meant one thing.

One simple thing.

Mutt spoke for the group when he turned toward Stick Dog and said, "We HAVE to get some more pizza!"

Stick Dog looked out of his pipe at the darkening night.

"Okay," he said. "It's too late to go tonight. But tomorrow night, we'll go. We'll try to get some more pizza."

Mutt, Poo-Poo, Stripes, and Karen began to hop up and down in excitement and anticipation. They knew Stick Dog could lead them to food. What they didn't know was this:

Stick Dog would not lead them to pizza the next night.

He would lead them to something completely different—and completely delicious.

And he would get help from someone they had met a long, long time ago.

CHAPTER 3

STRIPES ACTS AS A LOOKOUT

The moon was a skinny sliver in the dark sky above the Pizza Palace.

"You guys stay here," Stick Dog said. Poo-Poo, Mutt, Karen, and Stripes were situated behind a guardrail at the edge of the parking lot. "I'll take a quick look in the window. Stripes, can you keep an eye out for cars? Give me a shout if you see one coming."

"You bet," Stripes said, and nodded. "You can count on me."

While Stick Dog sprinted across the empty parking lot, the other dogs did all the things that they did best.

Karen chased her tail.

And didn't catch it.

Stripes watched her.

Mutt shook out that half slipper from his fur and began to chew on it.

Stripes watched him too.

Poo-Poo bumped his forehead a few times against the guardrail.

"What are you doing?" Stripes asked Poo-Poo. She watched him as well.

"Just warming up," Poo-Poo answered, before bumping his head again. The guardrail made a heavy, metallic, ringing *THUD-D-D.* "You never know when some good head-bashing will come in handy during one of our adventures."

Stripes nodded. This seemed to make

perfectly good sense to her—and she had no more questions about it. But she did have one more question for the group.

"Why is Stick Dog coming back already?"

Karen stopped chasing her tail—and not catching it.

Mutt stopped chewing on that slipper.

And Poo-Poo ceased hitting his head on purpose.

They stared out across the parking lot, and, sure enough, Stick Dog was on his way back. He moved fast, kicking up loose pebbles and small blacktop fragments with his paws as he sprinted. When he reached the guardrail, Stick Dog skidded to slow his momentum and then ducked under it to join his friends.

It was just then that a car pulled into the Pizza Palace parking lot.

"Stick Dog?" said Stripes calmly.

He was nearly out of breath, but Stick Dog did manage to answer. "Yes?" he panted.

"There's a car coming."

Stick Dog closed his eyes slowly, took several calming breaths the best he could, and then responded after opening them again.

"I know," Stick Dog said. "That's why I hustled back here. I heard it coming. The motor got louder and louder. I didn't want to get seen. Or caught. Or hit by the car."

"Good thinking," said Stripes.

Stick Dog couldn't help himself. He had to ask.

"Weren't you supposed to be my lookout?" he asked Stripes. "You know, to, umm, warn me if a car was coming?"

"Yes. Yes, I was," answered Stripes. "And I did. Just now. Didn't you hear me? I said, 'There's a car coming.'"

"Oh, okay," Stick Dog said. "Did you not

hear it coming? You didn't hear the motor?"

"Stick Dog," Stripes said. She seemed annoyed to have to explain something to him. "You asked me to keep my *eyes* open. You didn't ask me to keep my *ears* open."

"Oh. Of course. Yes, I see," Stick Dog said. He had fully caught his breath now. "I don't know what I was thinking."

Stripes said, "Maybe you weren't thinking at all."

"Stick Dog!"

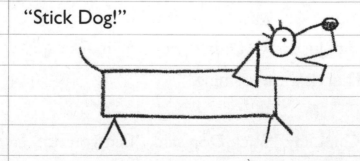

It was Karen. She was excited about something.

"Yes, Karen?"

"I almost caught my tail this time!" she exclaimed. "I mean, it was right there! Right in front of me. So close! I lunged at it and snapped at it. And right when I lunged at it, my tail got farther away. But, man, I'm telling you, I was super-close!"

"Good for you, Karen," Stick Dog said, and grinned.

"Why do you think that happens?" Karen asked. "Why does it get just out of reach right at the very last possible second? Do you know?"

Stick Dog did indeed know why. But he didn't think now was the right time to explain it.

"Let me think about it for a little while," Stick Dog answered. He then turned his head back to the parking lot. "This might be the Pizza Palace's delivery car. It might even be the same delivery girl from last time. With any luck, we might be able to snatch a pizza pretty soon."

This, as you can probably guess, grabbed all their attention immediately.

The car parked in front of the Pizza Palace. A few seconds later, someone got out of the car.

It was not the delivery girl.

It was a male human with a long neck.

Then a second
person got out.

It wasn't the delivery
girl either.

It was a different
female human.

"It's not the delivery car," Stick Dog said, and
hung his head a little bit. "Or the delivery
girl."

Mutt, Poo-Poo, and Karen hung their
heads a bit too.

But Stripes did not.

Do you know why?

I'll tell you. It's an important part of the story, after all.

Something caught Stripes's eye.

There was a slight movement
from inside the car. In the back window.
Stripes saw it. Her eyes flashed open.

Stripes said just one thing.

She said it loud.

She said it with absolute joy in her voice.

She screamed, "Look who it is!"

CHAPTER 4

STICK CAT IS IN HER SPOT

"It's Stick Cat!" Stripes screamed.

Stick Dog was startled by what Stripes yelled. He looked inside the car. And he remembered back to the time they had snatched five whole pizzas from this very place. Back then, they had discovered a kitten inside a moving van.

It all happened in *Stick Dog Chases a Pizza*, the third Stick Dog story. It is one of my English teacher's favorites.

In that story, the dogs— especially Stripes—got all freaked-out and thought the kitten was trapped inside the moving van. There was this big debate about whether cats were enemies or not—and should they rescue this kitten. Then Stripes got a real good look at him and saw how cute he was.

And Stripes declared the kitten to be her soul mate. And named him Stick Cat in honor of Stick Dog.

There's a lot more to it than that, but those are the basics you need to know for where we are in *this* story.

In this story, the cat inside this car did indeed resemble the kitten from back then. It was just bigger. It seemed odd to Stick Dog to see the same animal in the same place a couple of years later.

"Why would he come back?" Stick Dog

whispered, more to himself than to the others. He wasn't absolutely positive that this cat today was that cat from before.

And while Stick Dog may not know why Stick Cat was here again, you and I get to find out right now. It's part of the story, after all.

You see, it started when Goose, the male human with the long neck, and Stick Cat got into his car that morning. They lived in the big city far away. Tiffany, the female human, and her cat, Edith, got into the car too.

And here's what happened.

"Everybody in?" Goose asked, and looked at Tiffany in the passenger seat and Stick Cat and Edith in the back.

"Everybody's in," Tiffany confirmed, and reached her left hand toward Goose. He clasped her hand with his right.

Edith saw this from the backseat, rolled her eyes dramatically, and said, "Gross."

"Okay. Off we go," Goose said, and pulled the car out of its tight city parking spot. He thought now would be a good time to review their schedule. "It will take a few hours to reach my old hometown. We'll stay with my parents tonight and then our wedding is tomorrow evening. After that,

we'll head to Picasso Park for the party.
There will be a buffet and fireworks. But right
when we get to town, we'll stop for a bite at
my favorite restaurant."

"Sounds good," Tiffany said. "What's the
name of it again?"

"It's called the Pizza Palace," Goose
answered. "The best pizza I've ever tasted."

"You would know. You are quite the pizza
connoisseur," Tiffany said, and squeezed his
hand. "You're quite the pizza expert."

Edith saw this and said, "Disgusting."

Stick Cat smiled, hopped up to the car's back
window ledge, and stared out at the big city.
He had been waiting for this experience

since he woke up. The idea of riding in a car thrilled him.

"Do you want to join me up here?" Stick Cat asked Edith. "You can see everything!"

"No," Edith answered. She had found where the sun shined into the car—a warm rectangle of light on the backseat behind Goose. She had already curled up there. "I'm going to take a nap."

She was asleep in less than a minute.

Stick Cat smiled down at her from the back window ledge and began to take in everything.

He had only seen the big city from the twenty-third floor of his apartment building. To see it now from ground level was fascinating. As they moved away from their building, Stick Cat saw the piano store at the end of their block. He glanced to the right and saw Hazel's Bagels. There were coffee shops, bookstores, restaurants, and newsstands. He saw hundreds of people on the sidewalk. Everything looked so much bigger down here.

And the sounds.

The sounds were bigger too.

The first couple of honking horns startled Stick Cat until he got used to their volume. He heard police whistles, people talking and laughing, a train clattering, and a truck engine rumbling.

And he heard Edith snoring.

Haunk-shooo, Haunk-shooo.

Stick Cat smiled at that familiar sound.

After several blocks, Goose turned the car left. Stick Cat had to squint against the bright sunlight, which now hit the back window due to the car's new direction. He was just getting used to it when he felt a tap on his right shoulder.

It was Edith.

"Excuse me," she said.

"Oh, hi," responded
Stick Cat. "I thought
you were asleep. You should see all—"

But Stick Cat couldn't finish his sentence.
Edith had more to say.

"You're in my spot."

"Pardon?"

"You're in my spot."

"I don't think so, Edith," Stick Cat said.
"You were down on the seat. I started off
here in the back window. I haven't moved.
Maybe you were dreaming."

"I wasn't dreaming," Edith replied, and raised one eyebrow.

"I was in the sun."

"Right," Stick Cat said. "And the sun was down there on the seat behind Goose."

"'Was,' Stick Cat. 'Was,'" Edith said.

"Now it's up here. My spot was in the sun. Currently the sun is up here. So this is my spot now."

Stick Cat just stared at her. He didn't know what to say.

"So?" asked Edith.

"Yes?"

"Are you going to move or what?"

"Can't you just join me?" Stick Cat asked. "There's plenty of room. I'll scoot over some to this side—and you can have that side."

"I don't think so."

"Why not?"

"I like to spread out."

Stick Cat glanced quickly out the window. He was missing all the city's amazing sights and sounds.

"No problem," he said, and hopped down to the seat behind Tiffany.

Edith jumped up to the center of the window ledge, curled up into a tight ball again, and closed her eyes.

Stick Cat stood on his back paws, pressed his front paws against the side window for balance, and took in the city sights again.

For three minutes.

And then Goose turned left.

And Stick Cat felt the warm sunlight on his back paws.

He knew what was coming.

"Stick Cat," Edith said. "You're in my spot again."

He moved to the opposite side, assumed a similar position, and stared out the window again.

Stick Cat saw more shops—restaurants, bookstores, cafés, and furniture stores. There were orange cones and barrels and flashing yellow lights close to the car. He heard heavy truck noises and the slamming pulse of a jackhammer getting closer and closer.

"Uh-oh. Construction," Goose said from the front seat. "Looks like a detour."

Stick Cat felt the car turn right and, after a minute or so, turn right again.

He felt something else too. He felt the
warmth of the sun hit his face.
He squeezed his eyes shut.

Stick Cat did not squeeze
his eyes shut because the
sun was so bright. He had
quickly gotten used to that.
No, Stick Cat squeezed his
eyes shut in anticipation.

Edith tapped his back. She said, "You're
doing it again."

Stick Cat turned his head toward Edith.

"I really wish you would stop moving
yourself into the sunlight," she said, and
sighed heavily. "It's pretty annoying."

"I'm not," Stick Cat said as calmly as he

could. "The sunlight is moving to me when Goose turns the car."

"I think I know what's *really* going on here," Edith said. You could tell that she doubted Stick Cat's explanation. She had her own theory. "I think *somebody* here just always needs to be in the spotlight. That's what I think."

Now, you might think this conversation would frustrate Stick Cat— or even make him angry.

But you would be wrong.

He enjoyed Edith's peculiar brand of logic. Only his best friend could come up with such ideas. She was special that way.

"The sunlight is all yours," Stick Cat said. He hopped up to his original position on the back window ledge.

Edith settled into her original—and sunlit—position again too.

And, thankfully, Goose did not turn the car again for a very long time.

Stick Cat watched as the big city got smaller and smaller—until it was completely out of sight. He heard—and felt—the rhythmic bumps of a highway. It lulled him to sleep.

And he didn't wake up until the car stopped in a parking lot in Goose's hometown.

It was the Pizza Palace parking lot.

Stick Cat woke up when Goose and

Tiffany exited the car and shut the doors. He stretched the sleepiness from his body, arched his back, and looked out the window.

Stick Cat couldn't believe his eyes.

Five dogs were gathered by a guardrail across the parking lot.

And they were staring right at him.

CHAPTER 5

STRIPES AND HER SOUL MATE

"It's Stick Cat!" Stripes repeated even louder. She hopped up and down and pointed toward the car. She was totally excited.

"Who?" asked Poo-Poo.

"Stick Cat!" Stripes screamed.

"Shh," Stick Dog said. He didn't want them

detected before they had a chance to get some pizza.

"Stick Cat!" Stripes screamed again—at a slightly lower volume. "My soul mate! From a long time ago!"

Stick Dog tilted his head and stared into that car window with greater intent—and concentration. It only took him a few seconds to erase any doubt about the cat's identity.

"It *does* look like him," Stick Dog confirmed. "I think you might be right, Stripes."

"It doesn't look like him at all," Karen disagreed. "We saw a *kitten* in that big moving truck back then. This one is a *cat*."

Mutt and Poo-Poo agreed, nodding at Karen's idea. Even Stripes hesitated for a moment to consider.

"What?" Stick Dog asked. He had heard Karen clearly. He just didn't quite understand what she said.

"The animal we saw a couple of years ago was little, Stick Dog," Karen explained. "A kitten."

"But that was a couple of years ago."

"Correct," Karen said.

"So this could be that same animal."

"I think you might be a little confused, Stick Dog," Karen said. She then slowed down her words as she spoke. She apparently thought this would help him understand. "Back then . . . it was little. . . . This animal today . . . is big. Little things . . . are different . . . than big things."

Stick Dog understood now. Well, he understood what Karen didn't understand— if that makes sense.

He smiled at her.

"I get what you're saying, but—" he began to say.

Karen interrupted him. "Did my slowing down help?"

"Umm, sure. Yeah. Thanks for that," replied Stick Dog.

"No problem."

"Listen," Stick Dog said. "What we saw back then was indeed smaller. It was a kitten. But it's been two years or more since that night. I think the kitten has grown into a cat during that time. And this cat looks really similar to that kitten. Same color. Same features. You know, just bigger. And we're even seeing him in the same place. I think this human must really like this restaurant or something."

"Kittens grow into cats?" asked Karen.

"That's right," Stick Dog said. "And I think Stripes is right. I think this is Stick Cat."

"If kittens turn into cats," Karen pondered, "then what do puppies turn into?"

Stick Dog turned to Karen. He was trying to think of how to answer—but he didn't have to. That's because right then Stripes did something that none of the other dogs expected.

Something sudden.

Something risky.

Now, with absolutely no doubt that it was Stick Cat inside the car, Stripes leaped over the guardrail and sprinted toward the car.

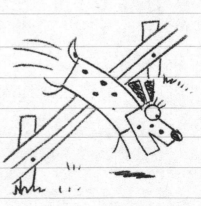

"My soul mate!" she screamed with sheer delight.

"Stripes! No!" Stick Dog yelled.

But he was too late.

"Stay here!" Stick Dog said urgently to Poo-Poo, Mutt, and Karen.

And Stick Dog took off.

CHAPTER 6

SHH!

Stripes got to the car in eight seconds.

"It's me!" she yelled at Stick Cat inside the car. "Your soul mate!"

Stick Cat saw her. Their eyes met. And when they did, Stripes yelped and began jumping, turning, and twisting with glee.

Stick Dog came up from behind Stripes in the parking lot.

"Stripes, calm down," Stick Dog pleaded. "And *quiet* down. Please. Someone is going to see us!"

Stripes stopped jumping, turning, and twisting. But she still shook and jittered.

"I'm just SO excited, Stick Dog!" she exclaimed. "I never thought I'd see him again. And here he is! Right in front of me! And he's still so cute! Do you think he remembers me? Do you? Hunh?!"

"You're not easy to forget, that's for sure," Stick Dog said. "I bet he remembers you."

"I think so too!"

That's when Edith popped herself up to the window next to Stick Cat.

"Look!" yelped Stripes. She started twisting and turning all over again. "He got married! That must be his wife!"

"I guess it could be."

Stripes began to wave frantically. "Do you see me? Do you see me?! I'm right here!"

Stick Cat saw her.

And waved back.

Stripes saw this.

And went nuts.

She sprang up on her back legs, flung herself high in the air, and waved her front paws frantically over her head.

"He remembers me!" she screamed. "He remembers me!!"

Then Edith waved.

"His wife likes me!!" Stripes screamed—and jumped even higher.

This had become too much for Stick Dog.

Way too much.

When Stripes landed on the pavement between frenzied jumps, he put his paws on her shoulders to keep her on the ground.

"I know it's exciting," he said to Stripes.
He held her still the best he could. "But you
have to calm down."

Stripes broke free from Stick Dog's grip—
and flung herself at the window. She was
suspended and pressed up against the glass
for a single second. She tried to smile at
Stick Cat—they were separated by less than
an inch of glass. With
her face pressed
against the window
like that, her smile
didn't look much like
a smile.

Then several things happened at once.

Edith shrieked and jerked away from
the window.

Stripes's eyes met
Stick Cat's eyes.

Stripes lost her momentary grip and slid
down the side of the car.

And Goose and Tiffany came out of the
Pizza Palace. They each had a big square
pizza box.

Stick Dog saw all these things occur almost simultaneously. He pulled Stripes around the side to the back of the car where the trunk was. He heard the humans come closer.

And he heard what they said.

"It's a good thing we called ahead," the male human with the long neck said. "I forgot that they close early on Thursday nights."

The female laughed a little. "I can't believe this pizza is so important to you. Is it really that good?"

"The Pizza Palace is the best," he confirmed. "The absolute best. And wait until you try Rocky's ribs at our wedding buffet tomorrow night at Picasso Park. They're the best too!"

Stick Dog gently put a paw over Stripes's mouth and looked around the back corner of the car. He saw the man open the door for the female human.

"Shh!" Stick Dog whispered to Stripes as softly as he could. His heart began to race and flutter. "Be as quiet as you can."

The man asked, "Should I put the pizzas in the trunk, Tiffany?"

That's where Stick Dog and Stripes were—by the trunk.

They couldn't run; Stick Dog knew that. The parking lot was a big open, flat space. They would be seen for sure. He had no idea what might happen if they were seen. The humans could try to catch them or call the police or the dogcatcher.

It was a dangerous situation, but Stick Dog was happy for one thing. His other friends were safe. Karen, Mutt, and Poo-Poo were still hidden far away at the guardrail.

It was right then that Karen whispered, "Why do we need to be so quiet, Stick Dog?"

Also speaking in a whisper, Poo-Poo asked, "Why are you hiding behind this car?"

Mutt asked quietly, "Have you seen the moon tonight? It's beautiful."

Stick Dog snapped his head around, saw his three friends, and whispered the most serious whisper he had ever whispered.

"Shh! Be still!"

They were going to be caught. All of them.

Stick Dog knew it.

He waited to hear what Tiffany—that was the female's name, Stick Dog now knew—would answer. Would the man bring the pizzas to the back of the car?

"No, Goose," Tiffany answered. "I'll hold the pizzas in my lap. They're nice and warm."

And Stick Dog's heart calmed a little as he continued to watch and listen.

"My favorite pizza tonight and then our wedding buffet tomorrow night at Picasso Park," Goose said as Tiffany opened the passenger-side door. "That's a lot of good eating."

And then Goose got in on his side of the car.

"They're leaving," Stick Dog said quietly, and removed his paw from Stripes's mouth.

As the car pulled forward and away, Stripes looked up.

Stick Cat was still in the back window.

Stripes waved and smiled at him.

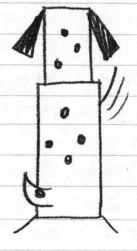

Stick Cat waved and smiled back.

Stick Dog looked toward the Pizza Palace. A man in a puffy hat was at the door. He turned the "OPEN" sign on the door around to its other side.

Now it said "CLOSED."

Stick Dog could not hide his disappointment. His tail drooped; he frowned a bit. He knew there would be no pizza tonight. Mutt, Karen, Stripes, and Poo-Poo noticed this, and their tails drooped too.

"There goes my soul mate," Stripes said. She appeared super-disappointed as the car moved out of the parking lot and onto the street. "I'll probably never see him again."

Stick Dog realized his mood was affecting the group. He needed to lift their spirits.

He started with Stripes. Stick Dog put a paw under her chin and lifted her head. He looked at her and smiled.

"You'll see him again, Stripes," Stick Dog declared.

"I will?"

"Yes."

"When?"

"Tomorrow."

That's what happened with Stick Dog and Stripes outside in the parking lot.

But something totally different happened with Stick Cat inside the car.

Stick Cat stared out the back window. He saw all five dogs. He watched as the sign went from "OPEN" to "CLOSED." He saw their tails droop. He saw the disappointment on their faces.

As the car moved farther and farther away, Stick Cat fully understood the situation.

"They're hungry," he whispered. "They must be so hungry."

CHAPTER 7

GOOD, BAD, AND GREAT NEWS

All five dogs watched in silence as the car with Stick Cat, Edith, Goose, and Tiffany inside disappeared in the distance. The car's red taillights grew dimmer and dimmer until they were gone.

It was then—and only then—that Stick Dog turned to Mutt, Poo-Poo, and Karen.

He asked, "What are you guys doing here? I thought I asked you to stay safely hidden at the guardrail."

"It's true, Stick Dog," Karen answered. "You did."

"Then why are you here?"

"It's Mutt's fault," Poo-Poo tried to explain. "He was fascinated with the moon."

"It's really pretty tonight," Mutt explained. "Just look at it. It's just a thin slice in the sky—and it has a pale-white glow. Kind of a silver hue. Can you see it, Stick Dog? It's such a unique color."

Stick Dog couldn't be mad at Mutt. He loved Mutt's sensitive side. He was the only one of

the group who would take
time to stop, observe, and
ponder the moon's color.

"It *is* lovely," Stick Dog answered after
observing the moon for several seconds. "I
honestly don't think I've ever seen that exact
color before."

"That's why I pointed it out," Mutt said. He
seemed gratified that Stick Dog shared his
sentiment.

"Thanks for showing me," Stick Dog said.
Then he inhaled calmly and added, "But
what does the moon's amazing color have
to do with you guys running over to the car
and joining me and Stripes? It was pretty
dangerous."

"Good question, Stick Dog," Poo-Poo said.

Then he scratched himself behind his right ear. "It was Karen's idea."

Stick Dog turned to Karen.

"You see, Stick Dog," Karen explained. "Mutt was so intrigued and fascinated by the moon's color, I just wanted to help him. He couldn't stop staring at it and talking about it. I'm very helpful, you know."

"Yes, I know," Stick Dog said. It looked like he was hoping to get his answer sometime soon. "So how does running to us at the car help Mutt look at the moon?"

"It's really pretty darn simple," Karen replied. "We ran here to get closer to the moon. When you get closer to something, it gets bigger and you can see it better."

"So, umm," Stick Dog said, and then stopped himself. He wanted to get the words just right. "So, did traveling halfway across the parking lot—What is that? Thirty or forty feet?—help you see the moon better, Mutt?"

"Yes, very much."

Stick Dog squeezed his lips together. Then he asked, "It appeared much larger, did it?"

"Much."

"It was about double the size," Poo-Poo chimed in. He had, by now, scratched away the itch behind his right ear.

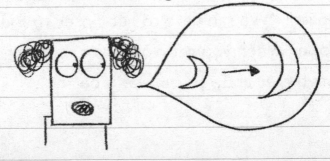

Karen added, "Maybe even triple."

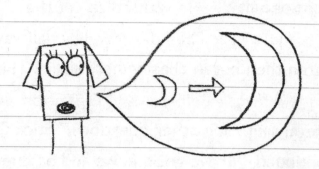

Now that they had provided Stick Dog with a clear and understandable explanation, his friends had some questions for him.

"Did you get any pizza?" asked Poo-Poo.

Mutt asked, "Was that really Stick Cat?"

"Will I ever catch my tail again?" asked Karen.

Stick Dog answered Karen first.

"I have no doubt that you will catch your tail again one day."

Karen then began chasing her tail.

"Regarding your other questions," Stick Dog continued, "I have good news and bad news and great news."

"Let's have the bad news first," Mutt requested.

"Okay," Stick Dog said. "We're not going to get any pizza tonight. The restaurant just closed. I heard the male human with the long neck—I think his name is Goose—talk about it with the female human. Her name is Tiffany. And the sign on the door says 'CLOSED' now."

There was disappointment on their faces.

"That's double-bad news," Karen said. She had already stopped chasing her tail. She hadn't caught it. "What's the good news?"

"It was indeed Stick Cat."

Stripes jumped joyfully up in the air, spun halfway around at the top of her arc, and landed to face her friends. She had been staring after the car this whole time.

"It was Stick Cat!" she exclaimed. "I saw my soul mate!"

"What's the great news?" asked Poo-Poo.

"There's going to be a buffet at Picasso Park tomorrow night!" Stick Dog said. "Goose and Tiffany talked about it."

He thought his friends would be thrilled

at this news, so Stick Dog was surprised when they didn't react at all. Then he figured out why.

He asked, "Do you all know what a buffet is?"

They nodded, but Stick Dog wasn't so sure they actually knew.

"Okay," Stick Dog said. "Mutt, what is a buffet?"

"It's a floppy hat worn by humans of German descent," Mutt answered quickly, and with great confidence.

"I believe you're thinking of a 'beret.' And I think it's French," Stick Dog replied kindly. "How about you, Poo-Poo? What's a buffet?"

"It's an arrangement of flowers that humans give to their smooch-kiss partners," Poo-Poo answered.

"Don't be gross," Stripes commented.

Stick Dog smiled. "That's a bouquet, I think," he said. "Stripes, do you have a guess?"

"It's not a guess. It's a fact," Stripes said with sheer confidence. "It's a gorgeous dance that involves lots of spinning on the tips of your paws. Like this."

Stripes then spun around once on the tips of her paws.

"That's ballet," Stick Dog said, and then noticed Stripes's disappointment at being wrong. So, he said, "That was absolutely elegant."

Stripes smiled and spun around again. She felt better already.

Finally, Stick Dog turned to Karen. "What's a buffet?"

"It's a little creature with pointy ears dressed in a red-and-green leotard,"

Karen answered. For further explanation, she added, "They help Santa at the North Pole."

Stick Dog hesitated for a moment before saying, "That's, umm, an elf."

"Same difference," Karen said. She didn't seem bothered at all that she was wrong.

Stick Dog explained, "A buffet is a whole bunch of different types of food."

"Food?!" Mutt asked in disbelief.

"Different types?!" yelped Stripes.

"A whole bunch?!" screamed Karen.

Poo-Poo just drooled.

"Yes. All of it's true," Stick Dog said, smiling at his friends' reactions. "The two humans that were in that car are getting married. And there's going to be a party or something at Picasso Park. That's where the buffet will be tomorrow evening."

"I know where Picasso Park is!" Karen exclaimed. She was super-excited. Her whole body shook with happy energy.
"I can lead us there!"

"Oh. Umm. Great, Karen," Stick Dog said. "But we've all been to Picasso Park hundreds of times. We go there almost every day."

"Oh, right!" Karen screamed. This fact didn't seem to dampen her enthusiasm.

Stick Dog added, "But you can lead the way if we happen to forget."

"I'm on it!" Karen yelled. Then she stopped shaking, pivoted to the left, and got ready to run. "Follow me to Picasso Park, everyone!"

Stripes, Poo-Poo, and Mutt all lined up behind Karen.

"Wait, wait," Stick Dog said. He was pleased that his friends were excited, but he needed them to calm down and pay better attention. "The buffet is *tomorrow* night. Not tonight. Remember?"

"Oh, yeah," Stripes said. Her shoulders slumped a little. "Tomorrow night."

Stick Dog decided to lift her spirits back up.

He looked at her and asked a single question.

"Do you remember who is going to be there?"

"Who?"

"Stick Cat."

"My soul mate!"

CHAPTER 8

ROCKET SHIPS AND MARRIAGE

The dogs had been to Picasso Park hundreds and hundreds of times.

But it had never looked like this before.

The gazebo on top of the hill in the center of the park was lit up. Strings of small white lights hung all around the inside and outside of it. Red-and-yellow flower arrangements decorated a dozen picnic tables inside the gazebo.

One picnic table was piled high with silver-
and gold-wrapped packages. Two tables
were pushed together longways. On the
tables were steaming silver trays, big bowls,
and baskets covered in linen napkins.

A smaller table had something tall on it that
was covered in a long white cloth.

"Where's Stick Cat?" asked Stripes. Then
before anybody could answer, she spotted
him herself. He was with Edith on top of a
table. "Oh, there he is! Look how cute he is!"

Stick Dog saw Stick Cat too. He said, "There
he is, all right. I'm glad you found him."

"Stick Cat! Over here!" Stripes screamed
from the woods. She jumped up and down.
"It's me!"

"Shh!" Stick Dog said, and lurched toward Stripes. He managed to get hold of her and stopped her from jumping again. "We don't want to be seen!"

"Oh. Right," Stripes said, and then remembered why they were there. "Where's this so-called buffet, Stick Dog? I don't see any food anywhere."

"I'm pretty sure it's on that extra-long table. They have the food all covered up to keep it warm, I think," Stick Dog responded. He was happy Stripes had calmed down. And he was intrigued by something else—that smaller table with the tall, hidden object on it. "I wonder what that is."

"So, the food is on the long table then?" Poo-Poo asked.

"I suspect so," Stick Dog answered, and stopped thinking about that unknown tall object. He turned to his friends.

Karen, Mutt, Stripes, and Poo-Poo stared at that long table and started to salivate a lot—and drool a little.

Mutt wiped some drool from his lips and

gazed out at the scene. The shimmering gazebo in the middle of the park provided a lovely and eye-catching spectacle. Mutt said, "It's beautiful."

He, Poo-Poo, Stripes, and Karen were all situated at the far end of the park—where the forest began. They were perfectly safe there, Stick Dog knew. They were hidden behind tree trunks, branches, twigs, and bushes. And it was dark. Only the gazebo on the hill was lit up.

"It *is* beautiful. But it's busy too," said Stick Dog. He saw dozens of humans milling around inside the gazebo. "This is not going to be easy."

"Sure it is," Poo-Poo said. "I've been thinking about it. And I know just how to get in there."

"You do?" asked Stick Dog.

"I do."

"Let's hear it."

"Okay," Poo-Poo said as the others leaned a little closer to listen. "All these humans are here tonight because of a wedding, see. They're not here to go swimming or to fly a rocket ship to the moon or to play in the sunshine."

"You're RIGHT!" exclaimed Karen. She seemed to realize instantly the logic that Poo-Poo used. "There's no water to swim in, no rocket ship to ride in, and no sunshine to play in."

"Exactly," Poo-Poo said. "They're here for one thing—to celebrate a wedding."

Then Poo-Poo stopped talking. He picked a burr from his fur and flicked it into the woods.

After a half minute, Stick Dog asked, "Is that all?"

"All what?" Poo-Poo replied.

"All of your plan?"

"Yes," he answered. He then picked and flicked another burr from his fur.

"Okay," Stick Dog said slowly. "I guess I don't quite understand."

"What don't you understand?"

"I don't understand the *plan* part of your plan," explained Stick Dog. "I get that the humans are here to celebrate a wedding."

"Because there's no water," said Mutt.

"Or rocket ship," added Stripes.

"Or sunshine," said Karen. Then, to explain further, she added, "It's nighttime, Stick Dog. Nighttime. There's no sun at night."

Poo-Poo said, "Everyone else seems to understand."

Stick Dog cast his eyes up to the night sky. He tried to calm himself by inhaling and exhaling slowly three times.

While he did this, Karen whispered to the others, "I think he's looking for the sun."

"I understand why they're *not* here," Stick Dog said calmly after his breathing exercise was complete. "And I understand why they *are* here. I just don't understand how we get the food."

Poo-Poo nodded. "I'll explain some more."

"Please do."

"It's the rules, you see," Poo-Poo said. "To be here, you have to celebrate a wedding. That's the rule."

"Okay," said Stick Dog. "And—?"

"And all we have to do is get married. When we all get married, the humans will have to let us in. That's the rule. Then we can eat all the food we want."

Stick Dog understood now. He didn't, mind you, think it was a legitimate plan, of course. But he did understand.

"So, we need to get married?" he asked.

"Right. That's all."

"Who are we going to marry?"

"Each other," Poo-Poo said, and looked around at the group. "It doesn't matter. I'll marry any of you. Karen, Mutt, Stripes. Whoever."

"I think you and I should get married," Stripes said quickly to Poo-Poo.

"Fine with me," Poo-Poo said. "Any particular reason?"

"Think of the puppies," Stripes said. "Whenever there's a wedding, puppies come next. I don't know how it happens, to be honest. I just know it's the next step in the process. And think how cute the puppies would be. They would combine my brilliant and amazing spots with your distinct and unusual puff balls.
They'd be so cute!"

"Okay," Poo-Poo said. "Makes sense."

Mutt looked down at Karen as Karen looked up at him.

"What do you say, big fella?" Karen asked. "Do you want to get hitched?"

"As long as the result is food, I'm in," Mutt said.

"That's so romantic," Stick Dog whispered, and smiled, but nobody seemed to hear him.

"It's settled then," said Poo-Poo. "Stripes

and I get married. And Mutt and Karen get married. And then we are admitted into the buffet and we can chow down!"

They reveled in Poo-Poo's plan for several seconds before Karen happened to glance in Stick Dog's direction.

"Hey, wait," Karen said. "What about Stick Dog?"

Thankfully, Poo-Poo had an immediate and practical solution.

"He can be like the rich uncle to both families," Poo-Poo explained. "He can provide for all of us whenever we need something."

Stick Dog grinned and nodded. Of all the parts in Poo-Poo's plan, this was the only part that actually made sense. But Stick Dog didn't say that out loud.

Instead, he said, "It's an amazing plan, Poo-Poo. For real. I can just imagine all those puppies everywhere. I don't know where puppies come from either, but Stripes is right. They are the next step in the process. And it's not just one or two puppies. It's often five or six or even more. Eight, ten, or even twelve sometimes."

Mutt, Karen, Stripes, and Poo-Poo quietly considered this.

"Let me think. Let me think," Stick Dog said, and paced back and forth in front of his friends for several seconds.

"What is it, Stick Dog?" Karen asked. "What are you thinking about?"

"Well, let's say Stripes and Poo-Poo have nine puppies in their family. Could be more, could be less. But let's just say nine. And let's say Mutt and Karen have seven puppies in their family. That would be a total of sixteen puppies. Then there's the five of us. That's twenty-one total dogs."

"Twenty-one!?" yelped Poo-Poo.

"Twenty-one," Stick Dog confirmed. "Twenty-one mouths to feed."

Mutt opened his eyes wide and shook his head a little. He muttered quietly, "Aye, aye, aye."

Stick Dog repeated, "Twenty-one mouths to feed every day."

"Every day?!" Karen asked.

"We have trouble finding enough food to share among just the five of us," Stick Dog said quietly. He appeared to be thinking out loud. "Imagine, just imagine, sharing that food among twenty-one of us. There would be some days, I'm certain, when there wouldn't be enough to go around. We'd have to feed the puppies first, of course."

The group was silent.

Finally, Stripes seemed to speak for them all.

"I don't care how
cute they are," she said.
"I gotta eat!"

Everyone immediately agreed with this
sentiment from Stripes—and that was the
end of Poo-Poo's plan.

Thankfully, Mutt had an alternative.

"I know what we can do, Stick Dog," he said.

"What's that, Mutt?"

"Well, it came up earlier during Poo-Poo's
plan," Mutt began to explain. "Remember
when he talked about sunshine and
swimming and rocket ships?"

"Yes, I remember."

Mutt wrapped up his plan quickly. He said, "Well, why don't we take that rocket ship and offer all the humans at the wedding buffet a free trip to the moon? Then, after the rocket ship blasts off, we'll have all the food for ourselves!"

"It's, umm, a good plan," Stick Dog said kindly and simply. "But there's no rocket ship."

"There isn't?"

"No."

"But I remember Poo-Poo talking about it."

"He was talking about how there *wasn't* a rocket ship."

"He was?"

"He was."

"So, there's no rocket ship?"

"No rocket ship."

"Jeez, I don't think my plan works very well without a rocket ship," Mutt admitted. "It's sort of the most important part."

"I'm sorry about that," said Stick Dog sincerely.

"It's okay," Mutt said. Then he shook half of an orange Frisbee from his thick fur and began to chew on it. This made him feel better instantly.

Stick Dog turned to Stripes and Karen.

"Do you two have any ideas about how to retrieve the food from the buffet?"

Karen did indeed have a plan.

And so did Stripes.

CHAPTER 9

NAILS—AND MORE NAILS

"Do you guys remember when we got those donuts?" Karen began.

Poo-Poo and Mutt said they did. Stick Dog and Stripes nodded.

"Well, I think we should use some of the things we used that morning. One thing, specifically," Karen continued. She spoke with pure confidence as she walked and talked in front of them. Her dachshund chest was puffed out; her stride was steady and strong as she spoke. "I think we should use that nail

that we used back then. Well, *nails* really.
A bunch of them."

"I have lots of nails," Mutt said. He shook
his back left hip and three nails, a bottle cap,
and an old orange marker fell from his fur.

Poo-Poo asked, "What do we use the nails
for, Karen?"

"When all the humans are sitting down,
we're going to sneak into the gazebo real
quiet-like," she explained. "We'll get under
the tables just like we got under the table at
the Tip-Top Spaghetti Restaurant."

"What do we do under the tables?" Mutt
asked as he tucked the orange marker and
bottle cap back into his fur.

"Here comes the best part," Karen said.
She stopped to look at them all. She wanted
to build up some drama for a few seconds.

Stick Dog asked, "What's the, umm,
best part?"

"We take the nails and hammer them into
all the shoes under all the tables!" exclaimed
Karen. She was clearly proud of her idea.
"We'll nail them to the floor! They won't be
able to move!
We can eat the entire
buffet. They won't be
able to do a thing!"

"I'm in!" said Mutt. He then began to shake vigorously to let loose some more nails.

"Great plan!" said Stripes.

Poo-Poo asked, "Humans have more than one shoe, Karen. Should we hammer more shoes to the floor—or just one shoe each?"

"It's an excellent question," acknowledged Karen. "I believe nailing one shoe will do the trick, but two would definitely be more secure. Let's nail two shoes per human."

"Maybe we should do three," Poo-Poo added. He liked that Karen had taken his thoughts seriously. "If two is better than one, then three is better than two. Should we do three shoes per human instead of two?"

It didn't take long for Karen to change her

plan further. She quickly said, "Three shoes per human. Yes! Mutt, we're going to need even more nails."

Mutt shook even harder. He had found four nails so far.

"Wait, everyone," Stick Dog said, and shook his head. He had to put an end to this as quickly as he could. The humans inside the gazebo were all eating now. As the dogs continued to propose and discuss their plans, Stick Dog had been keeping an eye on the happenings. He decided not to mention that they couldn't hammer three feet to the floor per human because, you know, humans only have two feet each. He tried a different approach. "We can't hammer nails into the humans' feet. They'll scream in pain. They'll kick at us. It will never work."

"Oh, Stick Dog, Stick Dog," Karen said, and shook her head. "You don't quite understand. We're not nailing their *feet* to the floor. We're nailing their *shoes* to the floor. Big difference."

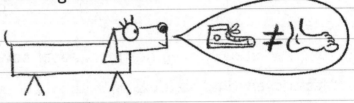

"Two more nails!" Mutt exclaimed after a couple more fell out from his right shoulder.

"Excellent, Mutt!" said Stripes.

"Keep 'em coming!" Poo-Poo said.

"Wait, wait," Stick Dog said with greater

urgency. "The humans' feet will be inside the shoes. When you hammer the nail, it will stab and pierce their feet."

Everybody stopped moving for a minute. They realized Stick Dog made an excellent point.

Karen wanted to save her plan. After several seconds, she had an idea.

"What if we aim the nail between their toes? That would make my plan work."

NAIL GOES HERE

Stick Dog said, "I doubt if we can be that precise. You can't really tell where their toes are when their shoes are on."

"What if we take their shoes off and examine the size and position of the toes?" asked Karen. "Then we could shift them around a little to create a nice big gap between their toes. Then we slip the shoe back on and—SMASH!—hammer the nail into the exact right spot!"

Stick Dog just stared at her then. He didn't know what to say.

For six seconds.

Then Stick Dog thought of something.

"Well, that might work," he said. "And I really admire your ability to amend your plan to fit the circumstances. Making adjustments like that is difficult."

"I'm very adjust-y," Karen said.

"Yes, you are very, umm, adjust-y," offered Stick Dog. "But I think we have one more issue that will prevent us from using your excellent plan."

"What is it?"

"We don't have a hammer," said Stick Dog. He did his best to sound disappointed.

Quickly, Karen snapped her head around to Mutt.

"Do you have a hammer?!"

Stick Dog really hoped he didn't.

Mutt shook his head.

"Bummer," Karen said. Her tail drooped down to the ground. "My plan was so, so, so close to working too."

"You're right, it was," Stick Dog encouraged. "But being really close is way better than being really far away."

"It is?" asked Karen.

"Oh, yeah. For sure," answered Stick Dog. "Would you rather be close to some pizza or far away?"

"Close."

"Hamburger. Close or far away?"

"Close."

"Ice cream. Close or far away?"

"Close!"

You could tell Karen was starting to feel better. Her tail was off the ground—and beginning to wag.

Stick Dog asked his final question.

"What about your tail?" he asked, and smiled. "When you're chasing it, would you rather be close or far away?"

"Close!"

Then Karen started
chasing her tail
with absolute glee.

She didn't catch it.

Mutt started putting the nails back into his fur, but Stripes stopped him.

"Not so fast, Mutt," she said. "I'm going to need those for my plan too."

Stick Dog squinted one eye curiously and asked, "What's your strategy?"

"It's simple, really," Stripes said. "Karen's plan spurred my plan. It really got me started."

"Glad . . . I . . . c-could . . . help," Karen panted as she turned rapid circles to catch her tail.

She hadn't caught it yet.

"What is it?" asked Stick Dog. He really wanted to keep this moving.

"Well, you know how Karen wanted to hammer nails into those humans' shoes, but it didn't work out?" Stripes asked.

"I remember," Stick Dog answered. "It was just a minute ago."

"Right," Stripes said. "Well, since hammering those shoes in place won't work, I think we should hammer their shirts in place. Instead of hammering their shoes into the floor *under* the table, we hammer their shirts right *into* the table. They can't move that way either!"

Stick Dog couldn't help but stare. He smiled encouragingly the best he could. It took him nearly a full minute to think of a response, but eventually he did.

"It's a fantastic twist to an already brilliant idea," said Stick Dog.

"Thank you. Thank you very much," Stripes said.

"And adding something to an original idea is often the hardest part of anything," Stick Dog said. "It truly is."

"What do you mean?" It wasn't like Stripes was questioning Stick Dog. It was more like she wanted to appreciate better his compliment to her.

"Adding something to improve on something else can make all the difference," he explained. "Does adding pepperoni to a plain cheese pizza make it better?"

"Yes."

"Does adding red sauce to spaghetti noodles make them better?"

"Yes!"

"What about adding meatballs?"

"Yes!"

"What about adding beautiful black spots to a white dog?"

WAY BETTER

"Yes! Yes!! YES!!"

"Now, you see what I mean," Stick Dog said. "By adding to an already terrific plan, you've really improved it."

"I certainly have!"

"There's still one small problem though," said Stick Dog.

"What's that?"

"We still don't have a hammer."

"We don't?"

"Umm, no."

Stripes jerked her head toward Mutt.
She asked, "Do you have a hammer?"

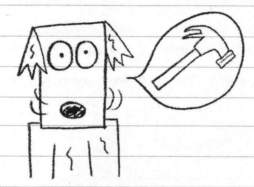

He shook his head.

Stripes turned back to Stick Dog and said,
"I thought maybe he had found one since
Karen's plan."

"Since a few minutes ago?" asked Stick Dog.

"That's right," Stripes said. She seemed suddenly sad.

Stick Dog was about to lift her spirits when a loud announcement came blaring out from the gazebo. It grabbed their attention.

And in just a couple of minutes, they would see something they'd never seen before.

Something beautiful.

Something scary.

CHAPTER 10

A FLYING OCTOPUS

Goose pulled a wireless microphone from
his back pocket to make an announcement
to all the wedding guests in the big gazebo.
His voice boomed out of a speaker that sat
on one of the tables. The speaker's electrical
cord hung down the table and ran to an
outlet in the grass. Something else was
plugged in there too.

"It's time for the wedding
fireworks, everybody!"
Goose said, and waved
his guests out of the
gazebo. After he turned

off the microphone and slid it into his back pocket, Goose looked at Stick Cat and Edith. "You two should come see this."

Goose then grasped Tiffany's hand and exited the gazebo.

Edith looked down at her plate. Just five minutes ago there had been several barbecue ribs and a heap of mashed potatoes there. Now, the plate was empty—except for several leftover rib bones. The plate, licked clean by Edith, now sparkled.

Stick Cat asked, "Are you coming?"

Edith examined her plate. She wiped her left paw across her mouth and said, "My work is done here."

Of course, the cats and wedding guests weren't the only ones to hear Goose's announcement. At the edge of the woods, Stick Dog and his friends heard Goose's fireworks announcement loud and clear.

"That's Goose," Stick Dog said when they heard the announcement. "I recognize his voice."

"What are 'fireworks,' Stick Dog?" asked Poo-Poo.

"I have no idea," he answered. He watched as the humans began to leave the gazebo and go down the opposite side of the hill.

About a minute later, a single thin streak of sparkling white-and-silver light shot up from a nearby hillside. It rose into the air in a slow, whistling arc. It had a brighter, whiter ball of light at its front—like a comet with a long, graceful tail.

When the streak reached the top of its arc, it exploded in the air. In a sudden burst, that bright white ball sprayed and sizzled out in dozens of directions, creating long pink and yellow tendrils of falling light. Mutt, Karen, Stripes, and Poo-Poo gathered as quickly—and as closely—as they could to Stick Dog.

"W-what is i-it, Stick D-dog?" asked Karen.

Before he could answer, Poo-Poo screamed, "It's an octopus!"

Stick Dog said calmly, "It's not an octopus. They live in the ocean."

Stripes yelled, "It's a new breed of flying octopus!"

"No," Stick Dog said again, calmly. "That's not possible."

Karen had a completely different idea. She said, "The moon exploded!"

Stick Dog shook his head and pointed up high and to the left. "The moon is right over there."

"Maybe *another* moon exploded!"

"We only have one moon," replied Stick Dog.

"Are you sure?"

"Pretty sure."

Mutt didn't say anything. He had lain down among the others and chewed on an old sock while he looked nervously up to the sky.

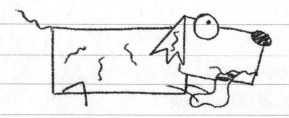

"These must be the 'fireworks,'" Stick Dog said. "That's what Goose was talking about. And I don't think there's anything to be afraid of. They're pretty, actually."

The other dogs looked up. With Stick Dog's thoughts and perspective in mind, they became less scared instantly.

Except for Karen. She still shook nervously.

Stick Dog noticed this and leaned toward her just a little bit. Karen leaned toward Stick Dog until they were pressed together slightly. This seemed to help her—she stopped shaking so much. Stick Dog made a mental note to himself to keep an eye on her during the fireworks.

"The fact that the fireworks are pretty is not the most important thing about them," said Stick Dog as Karen continued to lean on him and the others observed the colorful light show.

Poo-Poo asked, "What's the most important thing?"

"Look at all the humans."

The dogs looked toward the gazebo. Most of the humans had already gone down the other side of the hill. The last few were leaving now.

"Where are they going?" asked Mutt as he tucked the sock back into his fur.

"They want to see the fireworks," said Stick Dog.

"So, why are they leaving?" asked Stripes. "The fireworks are right here."

"They're not leaving all the way," Stick Dog replied. There was a hint of happiness in his voice—as if they were about to get a great opportunity. "They're just leaving the gazebo. See? They're going down the opposite side of the hill."

Karen asked, "Why are they leaving the gazebo?"

"Because the roof is blocking their view of the sky," he explained fully. "They can't see the fireworks from inside."

"What's so important about that?" asked
Poo-Poo.

Stick Dog grinned as a brilliant blue
spectacle of light burst high in the sky.
He said just one thing.

"Nobody is watching the food."

CHAPTER 11

KAREN CRIES A LITTLE

In less than two minutes, the dogs crossed the field, climbed the hill, entered the gazebo, and hopped up onto the buffet table to begin gorging themselves on all the food.

As his friends ate, Stick Dog crossed the gazebo floor, weaving among the cloth-covered picnic tables until he reached the opposite side. Stealthily, he looked down the hill. All the humans were there. Even Stick Cat and his gray friend were there. They were all mesmerized by the spectacular fireworks show. Their heads were tilted skyward in anticipation of the next colorful explosion.

Stick Dog felt certain about one thing: as long as the fireworks continued, no human would come back. He hustled back to his friends, hopped up onto the table, and felt his heart warm with pleasure. Mutt, Karen, Stripes, and Poo-Poo were chowing down.

Karen's face was buried in one side of a long, deep, silver tray of mashed potatoes. Mutt had found the potatoes too. He had just taken two seconds to lift his head out of the white heap of food. Melted butter dripped from his whiskers. He inhaled—and plunged his head back into the potatoes.

Poo-Poo and Stripes sat back and held barbecue ribs up between their front paws and gnawed tender meat off the bones.

Stick Dog saw a big tray full of leaves, tomatoes, and other natural things. He and his friends had foraged for similar items before. He saw dinner rolls that looked— and smelled—similar to the hamburger and hot dog buns they had often found. But it was the barbecue ribs and mashed potatoes that his friends had rightfully zeroed in on.

And Stick Dog joined them.

He went to the potatoes first. But after several delicious bites and gulps, Stick Dog stopped eating.

So did Mutt, Karen, and Stripes.

That's because Poo-Poo had something to say.

Before he spoke, however, another giant *Boom!* came from the sky, and Karen screamed, "What the HECK was that?!"

"The fireworks," answered Stick Dog. "We're going to keep hearing those big noises for a while, I think."

"You're sure that's what it is?"

"I'm sure."

"Not a cannon? Or a thunderstorm?!"

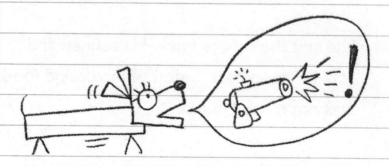

"I'm sure."

"It's not the end of the world as we know it?" Karen asked urgently as her eyelashes fluttered nervously. She wanted to be certain. "Everything's going to be okay? You're fine with all this booming everywhere around us?"

"It's not the end of the world as we know it," Stick Dog answered calmly. "And I feel fine."

Karen seemed satisfied with Stick Dog's response, nodded, and then turned to Poo-Poo.

She and the others knew his refined and sophisticated description of newfound food was not to be missed.

"This unassuming, curved, sticklike object is a delightful surprise," Poo-Poo began. A drop of barbecue sauce dripped from his chin. He held a single rib up in the air and turned it, eyeing it closely. "There's definitely meat here. It's tender and warm, and it's a great pleasure to pull and tear at it. It provides awesome gnawing satisfaction. But it's the brown sauce that makes the dish. It's truly spectacular, leaving a sweet, tangy, tingly, slightly spicy finish on the back of my palate."

"What is it, Poo-Poo?" asked Karen.

"It's familiar—very familiar," Poo-Poo answered, and licked his lips for additional evidence. "I get hints of brown sugar, pepper, and paprika. I taste tomato, vinegar, and Worcestershire sauce too. They all combine to make a thick, aromatic, scrumptious— and familiar—taste sensation."

Poo-Poo snapped his head down just then. "I know what this flavor is!"

"What is it?" asked Stripes.

"It tastes like Karen's favorite potato chips."

Karen squealed. "It tastes like *barbecue* potato chips! Are you kidding me?!

But with meat?!
Barbecue and
meat together?!"

Poo-Poo nodded.

"This might be,"
Karen said, and paused. It was difficult to
tell for sure—what with the lighting in the
gazebo and all—but it looked as if tears
welled up in little Karen's eyes just then.
"This might be the greatest day since January
sixteenth."

"The one day when you caught your tail?"
Stick Dog asked.

Karen nodded and wiped the corners of her eyes with the back of her left front paw.

Then she pushed off the table with her mighty dachshund leg muscles and soared through the air. She landed right next to the tray of ribs—and plunged her head into the sweet, tangy barbecue sauce.

While she did that, Poo-Poo returned to his description.

"There's more," Poo-Poo teased. "There's one thing more."

Stick Dog turned his head to ensure the fireworks show was still happening. It was. He then asked, "What is it, Poo-Poo?"

"After you tear the meat off and lick all the

sauce, there's a tantalizing final treat. A great finishing tribute to the dish."

"What is it?" asked Stripes.

Poo-Poo paused four seconds and then whispered, "A bone."

"A bone?" Stripes asked. You could tell she didn't quite know what to make of this new information.

Stick Dog tried to help. He said, "Dogs love bones."

"I see," Stripes said, but she didn't seem to

comprehend the relevance just yet. She didn't quite make the connection.

Stick Dog helped some more. He added, "And *you're* a dog."

"That's right. I am," Stripes said slowly. After a few seconds, her head gave a slight jerk. Her body trembled. She got it now. "I'll love bones!"

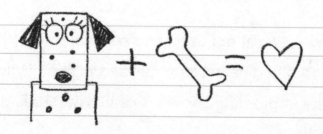

Stick Dog nodded, and Stripes grabbed a rib and licked and gnawed at it with terrific enthusiasm. You could tell she was anxious to get to the bone part of this newfangled food.

There were plenty of things on the long
buffet tables, including mashed potatoes,
salad, and soft bread rolls. But after Poo-
Poo's excellent—and savory—description,
barbecue ribs were the only food items
on any of their minds. Even Stick Dog,
after peering into the sky to guarantee the
fireworks show continued, took a spot
along the massive tray of ribs and snatched
one to enjoy with his friends.

For several minutes, the red, yellow, white,
and blue fireworks exploded in the black
sky in dazzling showers of bright, sizzling
light.

And for several minutes, each dog
devoured a rib.

And another rib.

And another rib.

And another, and another, and another.

Only one snippet of conversation interrupted their feast.

"We're totally safe, right, Stick Dog?" asked Stripes after her third rib. She didn't seem frightened or concerned at all. It was more like she wanted to have as much time as possible with those barbecue ribs.

"It's fine," Stick Dog assured. He had been glancing up at the sky and listening for the whistling sound of soaring firework rockets. "As long as the fireworks are happening, no humans will see us."

Stripes smiled and shoved her head into the

tray to grab another rib.

And Stick Dog was absolutely right.

No human would see them.

But somebody else would.

CHAPTER 12

SOMEONE SPOTS STICK DOG

Now, Stick Dog and his friends were in the gazebo at the top of the hill. And the humans and the cats were at the bottom of the hill. The fireworks continued to explode high in the sky. Stick Dog knew they were safe.

What he didn't know was that Edith was about to play a trick on Stick Cat. And that trick would jeopardize the dogs' entire mission.

Here's what happened.

Stick Cat stared into the sky with absolute wonder. His whole life—well, the part of his life he could mostly remember—had been spent on the twenty-third floor of a tall apartment building in the big city.

He loved to sit on the windowsill and stare out at the city. It was always so busy with sights and sounds. Flashing signs lit up everywhere. Traffic moved, slowed, and paused, and then moved again like a living thing. Sunlight flashed and reflected against thousands of windows on dozens of buildings.

But there was one thing he didn't see much of from that windowsill perch.

The sky.

Although he could see patches of sky here and there between skyscrapers, factories, and apartment towers, he had never seen the sky's great expanse.

But he did now. He saw black sky in every direction. He saw the silver sliver of the moon. And every thirty seconds one of those amazing explosions of colorful light would splash across that blackness, fade away, and reveal the darkness again.

"It's amazing, isn't it?"
Stick Cat said to Edith.

"What's that?" Edith mumbled.

"It's amazing, don't you think?" Stick Cat repeated. "The sky, the stars, the colors, everything."

"I *was* sleeping," Edith sighed, and yawned.

"Sorry."

"There's nothing like a nap after a huge meal," Edith said. She didn't seem annoyed. It appeared as if this catnap had refreshed her a bit. She pushed herself up and arched her back to stretch. "I *love* a good snooze with a full tummy."

Stick Cat smiled.

"There's only one thing that would make this evening even better," Edith commented.

"Mm-hmm?" Stick Cat semi-answered. Honestly, he was only half listening to his best friend. He focused mainly on the sky and the fireworks.

Edith noticed that he wasn't giving her his full attention.

She huffed and then said, "I *said*, there's only one thing that would make this evening even better."

Stick Cat heard that huff. He had heard it before. And he knew what it meant. He turned and, this time, focused intently on Edith.

"What is it?" he asked politely. "What

would make this better?"

"An after-dinner treat," Edith answered.

Stick Cat nodded. "I suppose it would."

"Like maybe another one of those barbecue ribs," Edith suggested. She pushed her back legs out one at a time as if she was about to get moving.

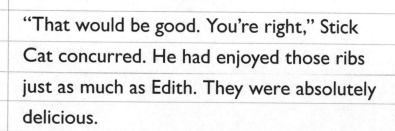

"That would be good. You're right," Stick Cat concurred. He had enjoyed those ribs just as much as Edith. They were absolutely delicious.

Edith looked at Stick Cat. The left side of
her mouth curled up a millimeter or two,
showing the hint of a smile. But Stick Cat
didn't notice.

Edith asked, "Would you like another one of
those barbecue ribs right now?"

"Sure."

"Great," Edith said, and plopped back down
to the grass. "Get me one too when you're
there."

"What?!"

"Get me one
when you go."

Stick Cat quickly understood what she had done to him.

"You want me to get you another rib?"

"Oh, I would never ask you to do that. I would never ask you to make a special trip just for me," Edith replied while she curled herself into a more comfortable position. "But since you're going anyway, sure. I'll take another rib."

Stick Cat shook his head and smiled. "I'll be back in a minute."

"Great," Edith said, and closed her eyes. "Wake me up when you get back."

Stick Cat started up that hill
toward the gazebo. On the way
he shook his head
again, smiled, and
said to himself,
"Only Edith."

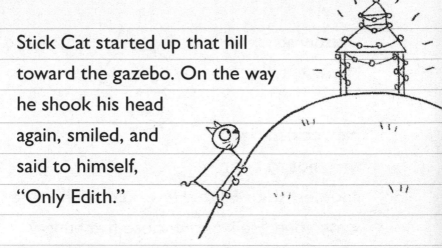

When Stick Cat got to the top of that hill,
he stopped at the edge of the gazebo.

He didn't go any farther.

And he didn't get Edith another barbecue rib.

He stopped and stared at five dogs on top
of the buffet table. They were all eating ribs.
They were the same five dogs from the Pizza
Palace parking lot.

"They *were* definitely hungry," Stick Cat

whispered.

"I knew it."

He decided right
then not to bring
another rib to Edith. He would tell her they
were gone. He wanted those five hungry
dogs to have them all.

Stick Cat slowly backed down the hill.

CHAPTER 13

GRAND FINALE

Rib bones were scattered all around Stick Dog, Poo-Poo, Mutt, Stripes, and Karen. The meat was totally gone. The thick, brown barbecue sauce was licked off them all. Wet with the dogs' saliva, the bones shone and glistened. The long, silver tray was now empty—and licked clean.

"What's next?" Poo-Poo asked.

Stick Dog looked left and right across the buffet table. There were plenty of mashed potatoes left, dozens of bread rolls, and a whole tray of tossed salad.

But something else had caught his eye again.
That table off to the side—that tall object
with the covering over it. What was it?

Stick Dog wanted to know.

It was more than curiosity that drove him.

It was instinct.

There was something under there.

He suspected it was something delicious.

He had to know what it was.

"You guys eat whatever else you want," Stick Dog said. "There are plenty of things to choose from."

"What are you going to eat, Stick Dog?" asked Karen. "I can recommend that puffy white pile over there. It's pretty good. Not as good as barbecue ribs, mind you, but still fairly tasty."

"I might try that in a minute," Stick Dog said. "I want to take a peek at that tall thing over there."

"I think I know what it is," offered Stripes. "It's that rocket ship from earlier. It's the right shape and everything."

Stick Dog glanced toward Stripes to see if she was joking.

She wasn't.

"Umm, I thought we decided there wasn't a rocket ship," Stick Dog said.

"*You* decided, Stick Dog. Not me," Stripes responded. "If it is a rocket ship, don't go flying off to the moon all by yourself. Make sure we get on board before you blast off."

"Okay. If it's a rocket ship, I'll let you know," Stick Dog said slowly, and turned away from Stripes and toward that tall object again. "I'll be back in a minute."

He was going to find out what that thing was.

But he never got the chance.

At that precise moment, Goose spoke into the microphone from the bottom of the hill. His voice boomed out of the speaker on the table, startling the dogs for a second. He announced, "Time for the grand finale!"

"What's a 'finale,' Stick Dog?" asked Mutt.

"I've never heard that word before," Stick Dog said. He thought about it for three seconds, then added, "It sounds a lot like the word 'final.'"

Stick Dog jerked his head around.

He figured it out.

"I think the fireworks are about to end!"

he said urgently. "The humans are all coming back! We have to get out of here!"

This announcement alarmed his friends momentarily.

"What about more food!?" pleaded Karen.

"What about the rocket ship?" asked Stripes. "And the whole trip to the moon and everything?"

"No more food. There's no more time," Stick Dog said. "And, umm, no time to see if that tall thing is a rocket ship."

"I'm pretty stuffed anyway," Poo-Poo commented, and rubbed his belly. He didn't seem to have a care in the world. "I ate a *lot* of ribs."

Mutt, Karen, and Stripes realized they were full of ribs too.

"We can take these though," Stick Dog said as he looked down at the rib bones scattered all about them. He calculated they had enough time. "They'll be good to chew on later. Mutt, do you mind?"

"Not at all, Stick Dog," he said, and spread his legs out slightly. He stood firm, proud, and still. "I'm happy to oblige."

Poo-Poo, Karen, and Stripes knew exactly

what Stick Dog meant. And they knew exactly why Mutt stood like that.

Quickly, they started to shove, push, and poke the ribs into Mutt's shaggy fur for transport. In just a few seconds, they had twenty-two ribs placed into Mutt's fur for safekeeping.

Stick Dog said just one thing.

And he said it fast.

"Let's go!"

And they went.

They jumped down from the buffet table to the bench. They hopped from the bench to the cool concrete floor. Mutt moved a little more carefully and slowly than the others to ensure none of those rib bones shook loose.

As they sprinted across the field toward the forest, a final barrage of fireworks exploded above them, lighting their way. Instead of one colorful burst every thirty seconds, fourteen bright fireworks blasted in quick succession.

"What in the WORLD is that?!" Karen screamed.

"It's the fireworks, Karen," Stick Dog answered as they ran.

"Are you sure it's not a hot-air balloon

exploding, two pterodactyls colliding, or
an opera singer who is really,
really, really off-key?"

"I'm, umm, pretty sure."

Karen seemed satisfied. She and the others
were now halfway across the field before
the sky faded to blackness.

"We can slow down now," Stick Dog said,
and looked back over his shoulder. The
humans were returning to the gazebo from
the other side of the hill. The fireworks

seemed to be over. "We're far enough away, and it's dark. Nobody can see us."

Karen, Poo-Poo, Stripes, and Mutt were all too happy to stop running and start walking. Their bellies were full; it had been an exciting, tense, and fulfilling evening.

Poo-Poo spoke for the entire group when he said, "I'm ready to get back to Stick Dog's pipe."

"It's not too far," assured Stick Dog. "We'll be there soon."

But it wouldn't be as soon as Stick Dog thought.

You see, just as Stick Dog and all his friends reached the edge of the forest, something happened that would make their adventure a little bit longer.

And a lot more rewarding.

After a quiet and dark pause of about thirty seconds, one last firework sizzled and soared through the air, curving to a final apex. Then it exploded in a sudden flurry of twinkling pink lights. A giant, shimmering pink heart took shape in the sky.

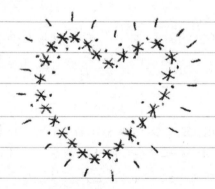

All the wedding guests looked skyward and applauded and cheered.

Stick Cat and Edith did not.

Edith groaned and said, "Ugh! Will this
lovefest never
end? I mean, really,
Stick Cat. Are you
as tired of this
romance-a-thon as
I am?"

But Stick Cat did not answer. He wasn't
listening to Edith. And he wasn't looking
skyward. Something had caught
his eye.

At the edge of the forest, a bunch of tiny
pink spots reflected the bright
pink lights from the
big heart in the sky.

Do you know what it was?

I'll tell you.

It was all the wet, shiny rib bones
protruding from Mutt's fur.

Stick Cat—with the keen eyes that all cats
have—saw those reflecting, twinkling lights.

And he saw the dogs as they entered the
forest.

He wondered if it would be the last time he saw them.

It wouldn't be.

Because right then Goose made another announcement.

A very important announcement.

CHAPTER 14

CAKE?!

Just as Stick Dog began to lead his friends to his pipe, Goose's voice—amplified by the speaker in the gazebo—traveled across the field and into the forest.

"It's time for the wedding cake!"

And Stick Dog stopped.

Mutt, Poo-Poo, Karen, and Stripes stopped too. They all yelped the same thing at the same time.

"Cake?!"

Stick Dog turned, fell to his belly, and dragged himself over some sticks, twigs, rocks, and dirt back to the forest's edge. He looked at the gazebo. He didn't think anyone had seen them cross the field and enter the forest. He suspected that all the humans had been gazing at that final heart-shaped firework in the sky.

But he wasn't taking any chances.

Not if there was cake involved.

"Did you hear that, Stick Dog?" Poo-Poo said. "He said there's cake!"

"I heard it," answered Stick Dog. "Try to stay down."

Mutt, Karen, Poo-Poo, and Stripes scooched low and fast on their stomachs to join Stick Dog. They peered across that field and into the gazebo just like he did.

The wedding guests now stood around the table with the tall covered thing on it. Carefully, Goose and Tiffany lifted the cover to reveal a massive, four-tiered wedding cake.

"That's a cake?!" Mutt asked in disbelief.

"It's beautiful," said Stripes.

"It's massive," Karen added.

And Poo-Poo said,
"It's time for dessert."

Stick Dog squinted
his eyes to sharpen
their focus. He had
never seen anything
like that wedding
cake in his whole life.
Most of their food was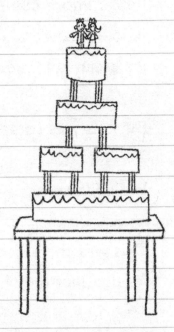
just scraps. They found leftovers in garbage
cans. They discovered food left behind from
Picasso Park picnics—crumbs and morsels
under the tables after the humans left. They
knew what cake was. There had been plenty
of birthday parties inside that gazebo over
the years—and lots of birthday cake crumbs
found under those tables.

Sure, some of their adventures had led to better, more complete things. They'd eaten whole pizzas and frankfurters and cartons of ice cream and mounds of spaghetti noodles.

But this was something different.

Way different.

This was the most magnificent and elegant food object they had ever seen.

And Stick Dog wanted to get it—and share it with his friends.

He just didn't know how to do it.

Yet.

And there was something else Stick Dog didn't know.

He didn't know that Stick Cat was going to help him.

CHAPTER 15

THE MOST IMPORTANT PART OF THIS WHOLE SHINDIG

At the edge of the forest, Stick Dog contemplated a potential cake-grabbing strategy.

Inside the gazebo, Stick Cat's best friend, Edith, did the exact same thing.

"What are those two people doing on top of the cake?" Edith asked from the gazebo floor. She stared up at the gorgeous cake and licked her lips and whiskers.

"I think they're supposed to represent Goose and Tiffany," answered Stick Cat.

"Humph!" Edith replied. She didn't like such an idea.

"What's wrong?"

"And what about you-know-who?"

"Who?"

"Me, that's who," declared Edith. "Why isn't there a beautiful cat on the cake too? A cat with a bow in her hair? A cat with a fancy collar? A cat with the most gorgeous, fluffy, and elegant tail in the world? I'm probably the most important part of this whole shindig."

"You are?" asked Stick Cat.

"Without a doubt. I'm really quite remarkable when you think about it," Edith said, and closed her eyes halfway for three seconds. She decided to pose a series of questions to get her point across. "Who's the biggest cat here?"

"You are."

"Correct. And who is the prettiest one here?"

Stick Cat knew how to answer this one. And he answered quickly. "You are."

"Who rescued Mr. Music?"

"You did," answered Stick Cat. In a lower

voice, he added, "Although I did play a small role myself."

"Emphasis on 'small,'" Edith said, and went on. "Who saved Hazel, the bagel maker?"

"Umm, you, I guess. But, again, I had something to do with it too."

Edith had already moved on.

"Who caught Tuna Todd?"

Stick Cat decided not to put up any further resistance. He just gave the answers that he knew Edith wanted to hear.

"You did."

"Who ate the most barbecue ribs tonight?"

"You did."

"Who ate the most mashed potatoes?"

"You."

"Bread?"

"You."

"And butter?"

"You."

"Well then, it's perfectly obvious," Edith
said as she wrapped things up. "I'm the
most special one here. If anyone deserves
to be on top of a cake, it's me!"

Edith then hopped up from the gazebo's concrete floor to the nearest bench.

"Where are you going?" asked Stick Cat.

She jumped from the bench to the tabletop and answered, "I'm going to take my rightful place on top of the cake, that's where!"

"What?!"

During this entire conversation, the guests had been watching Goose and Tiffany cut the first several slices of wedding cake from the largest layer at the bottom. They set each slice on a separate plate on a nearby table.

The guests were gathered around them, chatting and laughing—and waiting for Goose and Tiffany to finish cutting the cake. You could tell they were anxious—just like Stick Dog and his friends—to taste it too.

They were all too busy waiting, watching, and anticipating to see anything else.

That's why they never saw Edith coming.

CHAPTER 16

SO BRIGHT—SO DARK

"What are we going to do, Stick Dog?" asked Karen. "How are we going to get that cake?"

"There are too many humans," Poo-Poo said. "We'll never get any of that magnificent cake."

Stripes agreed. "It's no use."

Mutt reached into his fur, retrieved one of those rib bones, and gnawed on it.

Stick Dog raised his head and stared into the

black night sky. He was deep in thought. The moon cast a dull-gray light across Picasso Park. He had to think of something. Anything. He dropped his head and looked across the field at the gazebo. The humans were all gathered around that tall, fancy, multi-layered cake.

"It's so bright in there," he whispered. The brightness stung his eyes, and he looked away. "And so dark out here."

It was then—right when Stick Dog looked

away from the brightly lit gazebo and into
the dark night sky—that the moon began
to disappear behind a thick cloud.

The night got
even darker.

And Stick Dog got an idea.

He jerked his head down to look at
the gazebo.

"So bright in there," he whispered.
"So dark out here."

Stick Dog stared into the gazebo. He
followed that cord from the speaker. He
found where it plugged into the outlet.

It wasn't the only thing plugged in there.

There was another cord. He followed it with his eyes from the outlet, across the grass, and into the gazebo. He saw that the second cord led to the first string of white lights. And that string of lights plugged into the next string.

And the next string.

And the next string.

And all the other strings.

"What are you mumbling about, Stick Dog?" asked Poo-Poo.

Stick Dog turned to his friends. They had seen this look from him before. One eyebrow was raised slightly. The tiniest grin began to take shape.

"What is it, Stick Dog?" Stripes squealed. She, like the others, suspected that Stick Dog had an idea. She began to hop up and down. "What is it?!"

"It's so dark out here," Stick Dog said. "And so bright in there."

He stopped and looked at his friends one by one. He was determined. He was confident.

"It's so bright in there," he repeated. "But not for long."

CHAPTER 17

EVERYTHING GOES DARK

It took less than one minute for Stick Dog and his friends to race back across the field. They ran in complete darkness, and nobody saw them. They stopped just short of the light shining out of the gazebo.

Mutt, Stripes, Poo-Poo, and Karen listened closely as Stick Dog whispered.

"See those slices of cake?" he said, and pointed toward the table where Goose and Tiffany had placed more than a dozen cake slices on small plates.

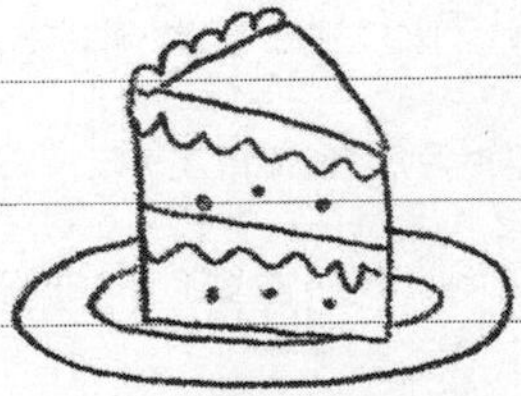

His friends nodded.

"I'm going to unplug the lights," Stick Dog said. He pointed to the outlet where the speaker and light strings were plugged in. "As soon as the lights go out, it will be completely dark. You guys grab a slice of cake each. Don't eat it here. Bring it back to the forest. It won't take the humans very long to get the lights back on."

Mutt whispered a question. "Won't the humans see us?"

"I don't think so," Stick Dog said, and shook his head. "It will be pitch-black. There's even a cloud covering the moon right now. And I think the humans will hold still until the lights come back on. You should be able to work your way to the cake without being detected."

Everybody nodded their understanding again.

And began to drool.

Stick Dog scurried on his belly toward that outlet. He thought he could get there and unplug the lights without being detected. He would only be in the light for a few seconds. And even if he was spotted, he hoped he could unplug the cord before anyone got to him. In the darkness, he'd be safe.

He was five feet away.

And still in darkness.

He paused to look into the gazebo a final time. He was right at the edge of the light now. One more inch and he would be exposed.

Nobody looked his way. The only unusual thing Stick Dog saw was the chubby gray cat on top of a table. She looked like she was about to leap off the table. From that angle, the gray cat would be able to see him perfectly when he moved into the light.

But, thankfully, her back was to him.

And nobody else was with her.

Stick Dog looked back and eyed the outlet. He got up on all fours, inhaled deeply, and scurried out of the safety of darkness—and into the danger of light.

Just as Stick Dog scrambled toward the outlet, several things happened quickly.

Stick Cat jumped up to the table to try to stop Edith.

Edith began to push off against the table with her back legs.

Stick Cat saw Stick Dog lunging toward the outlet.

Stick Dog reached for the plug.

Stick Cat reached for Edith.

Edith leaped for the top of the cake.

Stick Cat just missed her.

Stick Dog pulled the plug.

Edith flew through the air.

And everything
went dark.

CHAPTER 18

EVERYONE GETS TO WORK

One second after Stick Dog pulled the plug, two distinct sounds emerged from the darkness.

The first sound was this: *SHH-er-PLAKSH!*

The second sound was this: *THUMP T-T-T GLOOSH! GLOOOSH!! GLOOOOSH!!!*

SHH-er-PLAKSH!

THUMP T-T-T GLOOOSH! GLOOOSH! GLOOOSH!

The first sound was Edith as she landed belly-first on top of the wedding cake. The second sound was that cake toppling over—and its layers landing in different places.

Now, there was nothing scary about being in the dark. It was a bunch of grown-ups—and they knew everything  was fine. And even the noises were not alarming or anything. They were just kind of strange—and wet sounding.

But when it is very bright one second and then very dark the next second, it can be startling.

A couple of the guests gasped. But most of them laughed. Nobody moved. They weren't frightened. But it was dark. And people don't see very well in the dark.

But do you know who *does* see well in the dark?

Dogs.

And cats.

And Stick Dog used that to his great advantage.

And so did Stick Cat.

"Hold still, everybody," Goose called out in the quiet. "The plug for the lights probably came loose. I'll get it. Everybody, just stay where you are."

Everybody held still.

Well, almost everybody.

Goose stumbled, bumbled, and tripped his way toward the electrical outlet.

Poo-Poo, Karen, Stripes, and Mutt darted into the gazebo. They wove in and out of the humans' legs—never brushing against a single one. They each reached up to that table and grabbed a piece of cake with their mouth. Karen had to hop up to the bench first. Then they headed straight back to the woods.

Stick Dog stalked his way to the edge of the gazebo. He watched his friends hurry down the hill with huge slices of cake in their mouths. He decided to give them a head start—just in case a human saw his friends and chased after them. If that happened, Stick Dog would try to trip that human.

That's what the dogs did.

The cats were busy too.

Edith took giant bites and gulps of the cake that was smashed around her—and smooshed beneath her.

And Stick Cat turned his head from side to side—he was looking for something in the dark.

Goose got closer to the outlet—and closer to plugging the lights back in.

Edith licked white frosting from her whiskers.

And Poo-Poo, Mutt, Karen, and Stripes ran across the field toward the forest—they were halfway there.

Stick Dog decided his friends were a safe distance away—and worked his way silently down the hill and across the field to join them.

As all that happened, Stick Cat found what he was looking for.

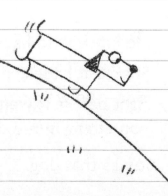

You see, when Edith lunged,
leaped, and landed on top of that elegant
wedding cake, it broke apart. The cake went
this way and that way and every other way.
Frosting splattered everywhere. The layers
tumbled and rumbled and rolled all around.

Well, except for the top layer. It collapsed
straight down to the table—with Edith
squished delightfully in the middle of it.

It was then that Stick Cat saw an
opportunity.

And he took it.

He knew who had unplugged the lights.
Stick Cat had seen him reaching for the plug
right before it went instantly dark.

It was that dog.

That hungry dog.

Stick Cat used his keen feline night vision to scan the gazebo floor. And he found exactly what he sought.

An entire circular layer of that cake.

It was smooshed a bit on one side, but it was mostly intact.

Stick Cat knew he had very little time. Goose would turn those lights back on any second.

And Stick Cat knew three other things too.

First, he knew Goose and Tiffany would not eat that cake after it had fallen to the gazebo's concrete floor.

Second, he knew those dogs were hungry.

And, finally, Stick Cat knew he could do something about it.

He took two quick bounds to reach that cake layer.

While it remained totally dark and all the guests stood still, Stick Cat pushed that cake layer out of the gazebo to the top of the hill. He could see that hungry dog nearing the bottom of the hill—headed to that same place in the woods where Stick Cat had seen all five hungry dogs before.

Stick Cat tilted the cake on its side—and took a moment to balance it. He knew how to do this—he had done it once before with a bagel sign back in the big city.

When the cake was balanced, Stick Cat did one more thing.

He pushed it.

Down the hill.

Toward Stick Dog.

CHAPTER 19

STICK DOG SEES TWO THINGS

When Stick Dog reached the woods, Mutt, Poo-Poo, Karen, and Stripes had their heads down. They were biting, chewing, and gobbling their wedding cake portions.

He smiled at them, knowing they were enjoying a sweet dessert.

He could smell the sugar in the frosting. It smelled scrumptious. He wished he could have gotten some cake for himself.

But he wasn't jealous. He was happy for his friends.

That's when the bright white lights inside the gazebo flashed on. It caught Stick Dog's attention. He snapped his head around.

And couldn't believe his eyes.

Stick Dog saw two things.

First, he saw Stick Cat standing at the edge of the gazebo at the top of the hill. He stared right at Stick Dog—and smiled.

Then Stick Dog saw the second thing.

An entire circular layer of that huge cake was rolling down that hill.

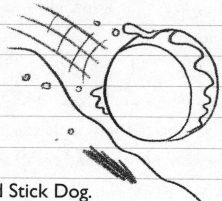

Right toward Stick Dog.

Stick Dog looked back up that hill.

But Stick Cat was gone.

CHAPTER 20

EDITH IS BUSTED

The lights flashed on inside the gazebo.

Goose and Tiffany screamed, "Edith!"

Stick Cat saw that hungry dog. And that hungry dog saw him. And then Stick Cat leaped back into the gazebo.

Now, when the lights in that gazebo came back on, one thing—and only one thing—

grabbed everyone's attention.

It was Edith.

She was right in the middle of the table—
and right in the middle of that top cake layer.

She was eating as fast as she could.

Tiffany, Goose, Stick Cat, and all the guests
gathered around Edith. She took a big bite
of cake, chewed, and swallowed. Then she
looked up.

She was covered in moist yellow cake and creamy white frosting.

Edith was busted.

And she didn't care one bit. She smiled a completely satisfied smile.

She looked at Stick Cat and asked, "Who is the most important one now?"

"You are," answered Stick Cat. "You most definitely are."

Then Edith plunged her head back down into the cake.

CHAPTER 21

STICK DOG STEPS ASIDE

That cake layer reached the bottom of the hill and stopped rolling about halfway across the field. Stick Dog got it and rolled it the rest of the way to the woods. Poo-Poo, Stripes, Mutt, and Karen hadn't seen anything for the past couple of minutes. They were way too busy—and way too happy—eating the cake slices they'd brought back.

They hadn't seen Stick Cat at the top of the hill.

They hadn't seen that entire cake layer rolling down the hill.

Stick Dog waited until they were done eating before speaking.

"You guys?" Stick Dog asked. He had placed himself strategically between his friends and the cake. They couldn't see it.

Mutt answered, "Yes, Stick Dog? What can we do for you?"

"I just wanted to ask you two questions," answered Stick Dog. "First, how was the cake?"

"It was so sweet," said Poo-Poo.

"And moist," added Stripes.

"It was amazing," said Mutt.

"Super-amazing," added Karen.

"I'm happy to hear it," Stick Dog said, and smiled. He waited a moment. He knew Mutt, Karen, Stripes, or Poo-Poo would ask him what the second question was.

He was right. It only took a moment.

Poo-Poo asked, "What's your second question, Stick Dog?"

"Well, I just wanted to know," Stick Dog answered slyly. He then took two steps to the left—and revealed the entire cake layer behind him. "Would you like some more?"

The End.

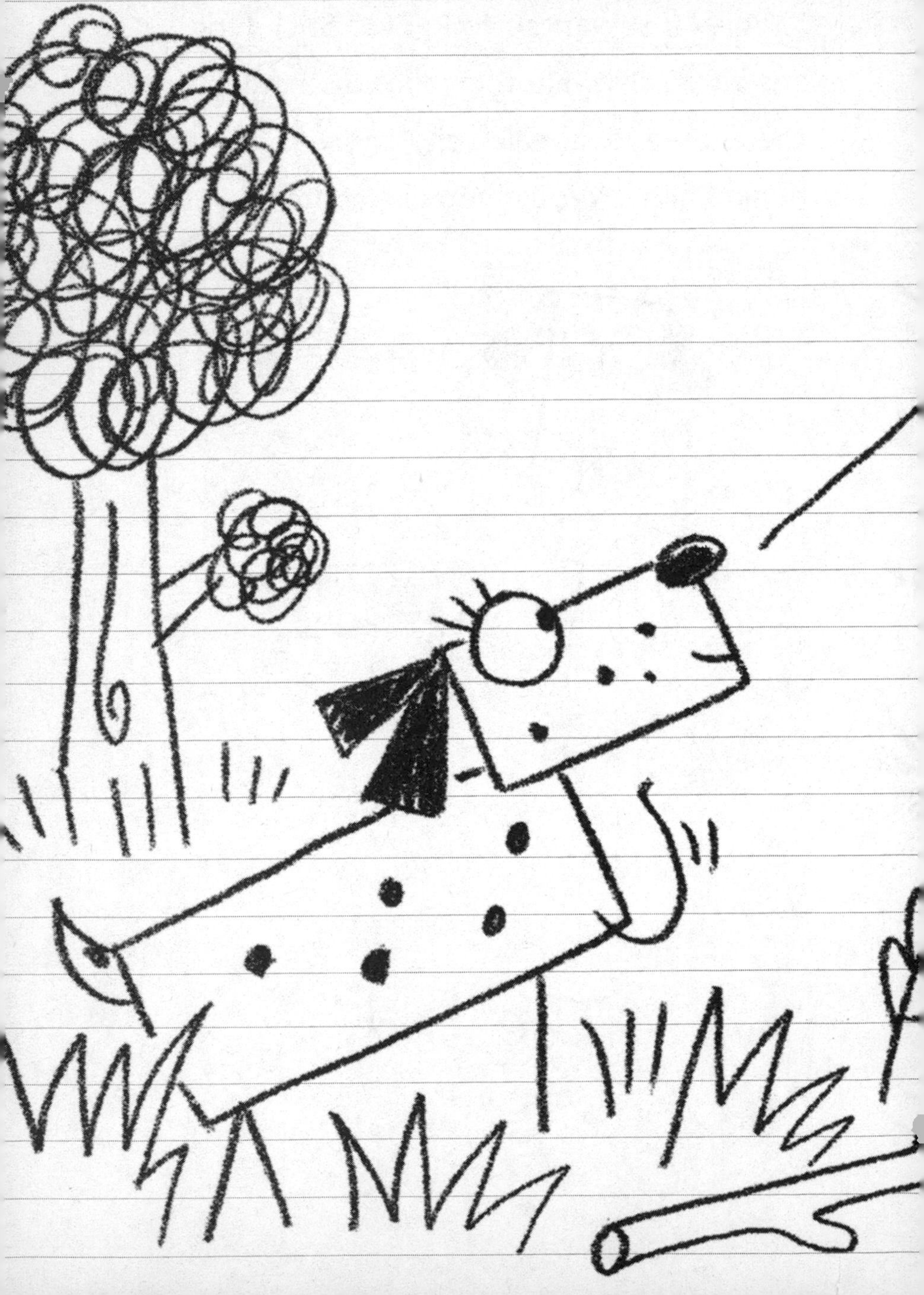

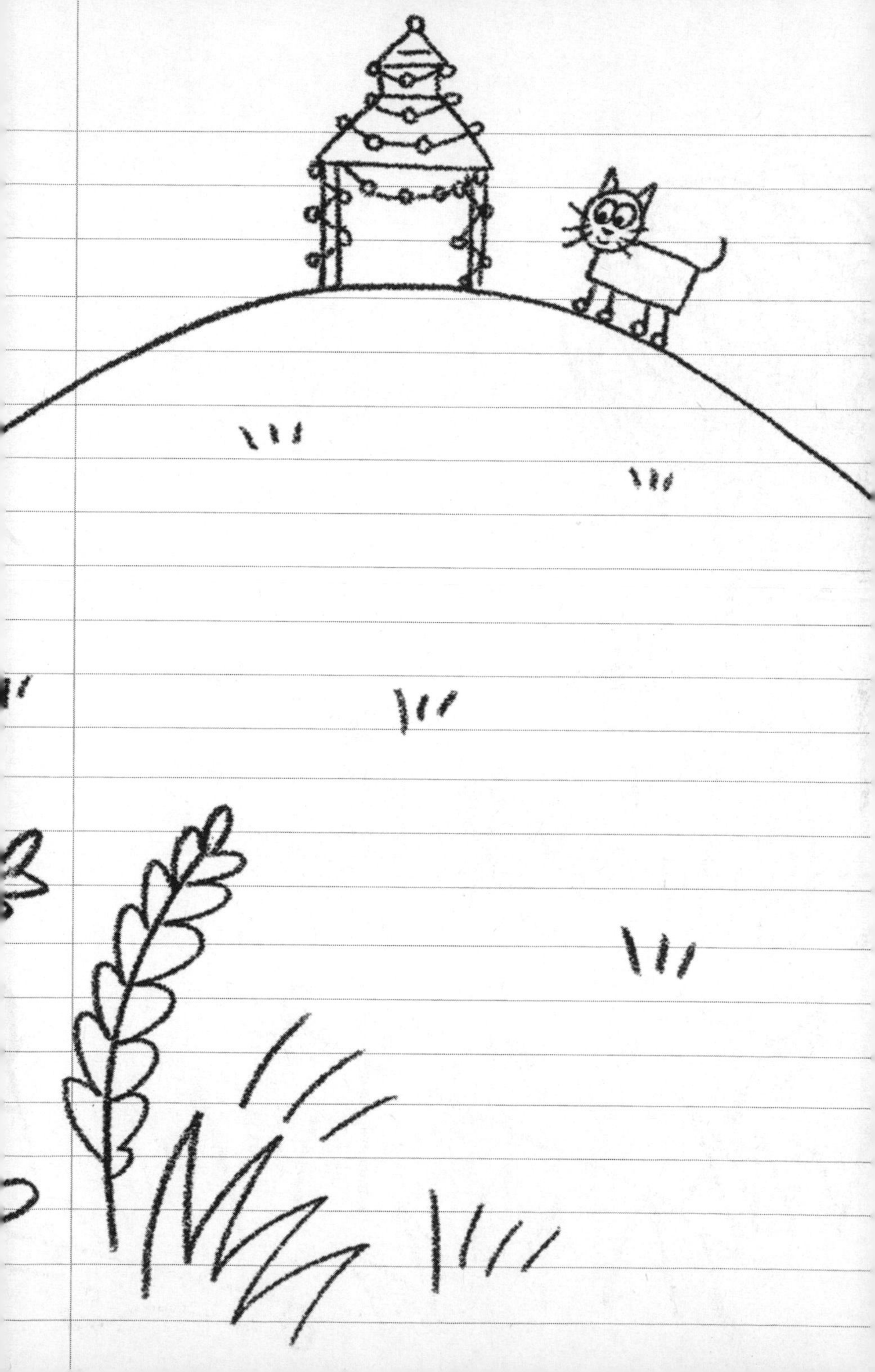

Tom Watson lives in Chicago with his wife, daughter, and son. He also has a dog, as you could probably guess. The dog is a Labrador-Newfoundland mix. Tom says he looks like a Labrador with a bad perm. He wanted to name the dog "Put Your Shirt On" (please don't ask why), but he was outvoted by his family. The dog's name is Shadow. Early in his career Tom worked in politics, including a stint as the chief speechwriter for the governor of Ohio. This experience helped him develop the unique storytelling narrative style of the Stick Dog books. Tom's time in politics also made him realize a very important thing: kids are way smarter than adults. And it's a lot more fun and rewarding to write stories for them than to write speeches for grown-ups.

Visit www.stickdogbooks.com for more fun stuff.

Also available as an ebook.